Praise for

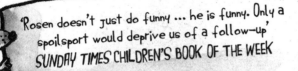

'Rosen doesn't just do funny ... he is funny. Only a spoilsport would deprive us of a follow-up'
SUNDAY TIMES CHILDREN'S BOOK OF THE WEEK

'Michael Rosen's wild story full of sharp-shooting humour, creative word play and a general sense of finely tuned storytelling anarchy is brilliantly matched by Neal Layton's illustrations'
GUARDIAN

'Ramshackle and silly in the best possible way ... Any smart young reader who likes having fun with language should like this'
FINANCIAL TIMES

'Reassuring and entertaining ... We'd expect nothing less from this industry treasure'
GUARDIAN IBW SUPPLEMENT

'Uproarious comic fiction'
BOOKSELLER

'Hilariously irreverent'
MUMSNET

a story in twenty-three chapters and two half-chapters (with helpful advice, helpful information, genies, baked beans, flashbacks, lizards, jumblies, weasels and mud supplied at no extra cost)

by

MICHAEL ROSEN

UNCLE GOBB
AND THE GREEN HEADS

with excruciatingly superb pictures full of helpful advice, weasels and baked beans by

NEAL LAYTON

BLOOMSBURY
LONDON OXFORD NEW YORK NEW DELHI SYDNEY

Bloomsbury Publishing, London, Oxford, New York, New Delhi and Sydney

First published in Great Britain in February 2017 by Bloomsbury Publishing Plc
50 Bedford Square, London WC1B 3DP

www.bloomsbury.com

BLOOMSBURY is a registered trademark of Bloomsbury Publishing Plc

Text copyright © Michael Rosen 2017
Illustrations copyright © Neal Layton 2017

The moral rights of the author and illustrator have been asserted

A CIP catalogue record for this book is available from the British Library

ISBN 978 1 4088 5133 3

FSC
www.fsc.org
MIX
Paper from
responsible sources
FSC® C020471

Printed and bound in Great Britain by CPI Group (UK) Ltd, Croydon CR0 4YY

1 3 5 7 9 10 8 6 4 2

For Emma, Elsie and Emile

CHAPTER 1

The Roar ...
(Or Is It A ROARRRRRRRRRRR?)

'... 23, 24, 25 ...' said Malcolm.

'Tell them to stop doing that,' said Uncle Gobb very loudly.

'... 26, 27, 28 ...'

'Oh for goodness' sake, Derek,' said Malcolm's mum, Tess. 'They can have a bit of a laugh counting their baked beans, can't they?'

'Beans are for eating, not counting,' said Uncle Gobb. 'I have one basic rule when it comes to eating: "Eat it, or leave it!"'

Malcolm looked at Uncle Gobb. He thought: the thing I hate most in the world is Uncle Gobb being here. The thing I hate next-most is having hair in my mouth. I've figured out how to get rid of hair in my mouth. So far, I haven't figured out how to get rid of Uncle Gobb. I've managed to bamboozle and confuzle him. But I haven't managed to get rid of him.

'… 32, 33, 34 – I win!' shouted Crackersnacker.

Crackersnacker is Malcolm's greatest, bestest, most brilliantest and terrifickest friend. They love thinking about that time they escaped from Uncle Gobb's **DREAD SHED** and bamboozled and confuzled him.

Malcolm dipped the serving spoon in the beans bowl and served himself some more beans.

Uncle Gobb leaned across the table and put his shiny face up close to Malcolm's not-so-shiny face.

'Are you going to eat those extra beans? Because if you're not going to eat those beans, those beans will be wasted. They don't waste beans in China!'

'Oh no,' said Crackersnacker. 'They won't be wasted, Mr Gobb. We'll play "Flick-bean" with them.' He mimed flicking a bean and did the sound effect to go with it: '**Pffflerk!**'

'**Pffflerk**' was Crackersnacker's very own invented bean-flicking sound.

Malcolm looked hard at Uncle Gobb again. He was bright red and panting in a shiny sort of a way. Malcolm thought that Uncle Gobb was so angry with him and Crackersnacker that he must be very near to exploding. At any second, he could blow up.

I wonder which bit of Uncle Gobb would fly off first if he started to explode, Malcolm thought. His ears? His nose?

'Tessa!' shouted Uncle Gobb at Malcom's mum. 'Do something! Say something!'

Mum said, 'It's Friday. I've said something.'

Uncle Gobb put his head in his hands and slumped forwards. 'I don't mean, "say anything". I mean say something about the boys' outrageous behaviour. This is about discipline.'

'No,' said Malcolm. 'It's about beans.'

'It could be about discipline AND beans,' said Crackersnacker.

'What? At the same time?' Malcolm asked.

Uncle Gobb stood up and roared.

Malcolm looked at Uncle Gobb yet again. He thought; this isn't good. This isn't fun. Roaring is what Uncle Gobb does when I don't do what Uncle Gobb thinks I should be doing. Well, if he doesn't like it, why can't he live somewhere else? Why can't he puff himself up bigger and bigger and turn into one of those balloons that fly up to the sky and float out of sight?

RoOoOoAAAAAaaaaa

Malcolm knew exactly why Uncle Gobb lived with him and his mum. It was because Uncle Gobb used to live with his wife, Tammy, but one day it all exploded:

BLAMMM!!

And so he had to come and live with them. That's what Mum had said. Or something like that.

But now it's hurting my head, Malcolm thought.

Uncle Gobb went on roaring.

RRRRRRRRRRRRRRRR!!!!!

'This is a long roar,' said Crackersnacker.

Crackersnacker often came over to Malcolm's house. Mum thought that he looked peaky. Malcolm had figured out that Mum gave him food so that he might end up looking less peaky.

So, because Crackersnacker came over quite often, he had seen one of Uncle Gobb's roars before.

THE LAST TIME CRACKERSNACKER
SAW ONE OF UNCLE GOBB'S ROARS

This is a 'flashback'. There will be several flashbacks in this book. Health warning: just because it's a flashback does NOT mean there will be any flashing lights. Nothing will flash. And nothing will flash back, either. End of health warning.

BEGINNING OF FLASHBACK

The last roar was three weeks earlier. Malcolm and Crackersnacker had not wanted to know the name of a spider.

(If you don't want to know about spiders, look away now.)

Malcolm and Crackersnacker had found a spider under the sofa.

Crackersnacker said that if you drop a spider it's just like Spider-Man; the spider makes a long thread thing and it just hangs around on the end of it.

EIGHT
LEGS

ONE
LEG

NO
LEGS

Uncle Gobb said, 'Do you know what kind of spider it is? If you don't know, you should be doing spider homework. They know the names of spiders in China. Does a spider have eight legs, one leg or no legs? Malcolm, do you know the name of the spider?'

'Peter Parker,' Malcolm said.

Crackersnacker said, 'That's brilliant, Ponkyboy. Lightning thinking!'

And Uncle Gobb roared.

END OF FLASHBACK

Just checking, but there was no flashing there, was there?
And no flashing back? I'm afraid that we couldn't show you a
picture of Spider-Man there but Spider-Man and his human self,
Peter Parker, can be seen on TVs, tablets and at a cinema near you.
That's what's called 'HELPFUL ADVICE'.
I am hoping that this book will be full of HELPFUL ADVICE
and helpful explanations. This will be FREE. At no extra cost.

Now, back to the longer roar. The one that
came after the discipline-and-beans thing.

Oh dear, it's still going on.

Malcolm was hoping very much that it
would stop. Crackersnacker was hoping it would
stop. Mum was hoping it would stop. The dog
was hoping it would stop. I was hoping that it

would stop. You're hoping it would stop. If there were any weasels here, they would be hoping it would stop. I'm sure weasels don't like roaring.

 Weasels: We don't like roaring.

Hang on a minute, weasels don't talk.

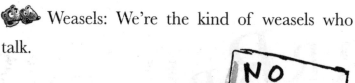 Weasels: We're the kind of weasels who talk.

That sounds like a **KILLER ANSWER** from the 'DICTIONARY OF KILLER ANSWERS'.

RrRrRrrRr!

'It's still going on,' said Crackersnacker.

There's only one thing for it, Malcolm was thinking. If I can't get rid of Uncle Gobb right now, all I can do is the *Dreamy Thing*.

The *Dreamy Thing* goes like this:
1. Something horrible happens. Like that raggedy bit you get down the side of your fingernail so that every time you put your hand in your pocket, it feels like someone is sticking a needle into the side of your finger.

If getting a 'raggedy bit' ever happens to you, let me recommend that you put a plaster over it. That's more HELPFUL ADVICE for you.

2. Sorry about the interruption in the *Dreamy Thing* list. The list will now carry on.

3. Malcolm is unhappy that something horrible happens.

4. Malcolm gets the *Dreamy Thing* in his mind.

5. In the *dreaminess*, a man with an American accent appears. He says, 'Hey Malky, buddy, don't worry about it. Let's go get something to eat.'

6. The man puts his hand on Malcolm's head. He ruffles up Malcolm's hair.

RrRʀRʀRRRoOOoOᴀᴀAᴀᴀ

The roaring was still going on.

Malcolm looked at Mum.

Mum knows how to calm Uncle Gobb down, Malcolm thought. He's her brother. She's his sister. That's why he came to stay with us. He didn't have anywhere else to go.

Mum looked back at Malcolm and then she looked over to Uncle Gobb and she said, 'I'd love a bit of chocolate, Derek. Could you pop out and get me a minty one? And get yourself some while you're about it.'

AARRRrrRRroOARRR

(In case you're wondering why Mum
didn't say, 'And get the boys some too,' it was
because Uncle Gobb said that the boys couldn't
have chocolate and they especially couldn't have
their favourite, which was a Crumbles Bar. So
Mum puts the Crumbles Bars in a secret store.
If you're wondering where the secret store is,
I'm afraid I can't tell you because … er … it's a
secret.)

Uncle Gobb stopped roaring.

He smoothed down his hair and left the room.

He came back into the room. He pointed at Malcolm, looked at Mum, wagged his finger and said, 'He's going to have to go.'

Mum said, 'Don't be silly, Derek, he can't cross that busy road on his own.'

'I don't mean that kind of "go". I mean the other kind of "go",' Uncle Gobb said and nodded seriously.

'Mine's minty, remember,' Mum said, ignoring him and his different kinds of 'go'.

Uncle Gobb left the room again.

Later, when Crackersnacker and I are in my room, I'm going to tell him about the *Dreamy Thing*, Malcolm thought. I've got a feeling that it's going to help us get rid of Uncle Gobb … I don't know how. Crackersnacker will know. But we better get on with it quick, before Uncle Gobb does something to get rid of me. I

know what he meant by that 'other kind of go'
thing ...

Without saying anything, Mum handed
Malcolm the key to the secret store, which is
beginning to need some capital letters:

The Secret Store.

Or better still:

THE SECRET STORE.

Hey, Weasels! Get out of there.

I don't care, get out of
THE SECRET STORE.

And here is a picture of Malcolm and Crackersnacker eating chocolate Crumbles Bars. They are doing it in such a secret way that you can't see the chocolate Crumbles Bars. But believe me, there are chocolate Crumbles Bars in there.

Here is some evidence that there are chocolate Crumbles Bars in there. It's what's called a 'cross section'.

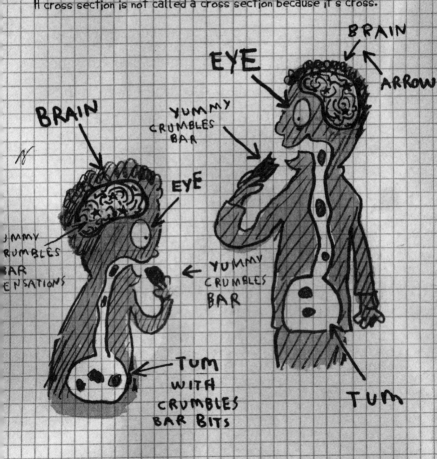

If all this talk about chocolate is making you want to have chocolate, I must apologise. This book doesn't come with free chocolate. It doesn't even come with a golden ticket which will let you into a chocolate factory. That comes in another book, called *Harry and the Chocolate Factory*.

If ever you read something in this book that you think is not true, stand up, make sure that you haven't got a wedgie and sit down again. That usually sorts it out.

CHAPTER 2

The Dreamy Thing

When Crackersnacker came over for a sleepover, he liked to sleep on a mattress on the floor while Malcolm slept in his bed.

'Do you ever get the *Dreamy Thing*?' Malcolm said from his bed.

'Yes,' said Crackersnacker from his mattress on the floor.

There was a long, long, long pause.

'Is your *Dreamy Thing* the same as my *Dreamy Thing*?' Malcolm said.

'I don't know,' said Crackersnacker.

There was a long, long, long pause.

'It couldn't be the same, very same, totally same, anyway,' said Crackersnacker.

'Oh,' said Malcolm.

There was a long, long, long pause. (From now on, you'll have to imagine these long, long,

long pauses. They'll be there, even if it doesn't say, 'long, long, long pause'. You'll just have to think them.)

'You see,' said Crackersnacker, sitting up on his elbow, 'yesterday I had a burger at Barbecue Bob's Burger Bar and you didn't. So you haven't got what happened at Barbecue Bob's Burger Bar yesterday in your head. I've got it in my head. You haven't.'

'What DID happen at Barbecue Bob's Burger Bar yesterday?' said Malcolm.

'Nothing much,'
Crackersnacker said.

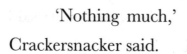

'What's your
Dreamy Stuff like?'
Malcolm said.

'Barbecue
Bob's burgers,' said
Crackersnacker.

'My *Dreamy Stuff* is about this man,' said Malcolm. 'He says, "Hey Malky, buddy, don't worry about it. Let's go get something to eat."'

'You said that in American,' Cracker-snacker said.

'That's because he's American,' Malcolm said.

'Is he?' Crackersnacker said.

'No,' Malcolm said.

'What it is, yeah …' Malcolm said. 'What it is, is … he's my dad.'

'Right,' said Crackersnacker.

'You know when Uncle Gobb does all that asking questions and telling us what to do stuff, and when he does all that roaring … ?' Malcolm said.

Crackersnacker was still thinking about the fact that Malcolm had a dad.

'Where is your dad?' he said.

'In America,' Malcolm said.

'Great,' Crackersnacker said.

'Do you think that if we went to America, we could get rid of Uncle Gobb forever?' Malcolm said.

'Yep,' said Crackersnacker.

'I don't just mean bamboozle and confuzle him,' Malcolm said. 'I mean really get rid of him, like we said we would.'

'Yep,' said Crackersnacker. 'We can do that.'

Malcolm suddenly felt good. 'Go on,' he said.

'What do you mean?' said Crackersnacker.

'Like how will we get rid of him?' said Malcolm.

'We take him to America and then leave him there,' said Crackersnacker.

Malcolm collapsed back down on to the bed. They couldn't just leave him there. What? Go to America and say to Uncle Gobb, 'We're going back now. You're not.'?

Or could they?

OR COULD THEY ... ?????!!!!!!!!

Maybe, they could go somewhere like the Grand Canyon and say, 'Look Uncle Gobb, there's the Grand Canyon,' and then run away.

'I was thinking,' said Malcolm, 'that my dad would do it. He could get rid of Uncle Gobb.'

'Yeah,' said Crackersnacker. 'Your dad would have loads of candyfloss and he would cover Uncle Gobb in candyfloss. And that would, that would … er …'

'They don't call it candyfloss,' said Malcolm. 'They call it "cotton candy".'

'Do they?' said Crackersnacker. 'How do you know?'

'Because when I was last there, I had cotton candy. My dad bought me some cotton candy.'

'And it was the same, totally the same as candyfloss?' said Crackersnacker.

'Well,' said Malcolm, 'it can't be the same, very same, totally the same, because the cotton candy didn't go into Barbecue Bob's Burger Bar.'

'How are we going to get to America?' Crackersnacker said.

'By plane,' said Malcolm.

'Great,' said Crackersnacker. 'Vroooomm.'

'I think you two need to get some sleep now, don't you?' Mum called out from outside.

'Don't ask them,' the boys heard Uncle Gobb say. 'Just tell them.'

'I did,' said Mum.

'If you think that's telling,' said Uncle Gobb, 'Barnacle Bill's a sailor.'

'Barnacle Bill IS a sailor,' said Mum.

Malcolm and Crackersnacker heard the way Mum just sorted out Uncle Gobb with that Barnacle Bill fact. They waved to each other in the dark, doing long-distance, not-touching high fives.

CHAPTER 3

Going To America

The next day at school, Mr Keenly was saying, 'Now then, we're thinking of situations when you might be getting giggly.'

Mr Keenly was using the white board. It had the words GETTING GIGGLY on it.

Getting giggly

Malcolm had read the words GETTING GIGGLY but now he was trying to read some other words which were at the bottom of the white board. He leaned forward and screwed up his eyes. He didn't do that with a screwdriver as that would hurt. And anyway, he didn't have a screwdriver with him.

He could just make out what the words said. They said, 'Gobb Education'. Oh no, not again, he thought. It felt like Uncle Gobb had followed him to school. It was like everywhere he went he was in Gobb country. And he couldn't escape.

The class were in their 'Talk Groups' and they were talking about 'GETTING GIGGLY'.

Malcolm's Talk Group was Ulla, Spaghetti and Crackersnacker.

 Malcolm: What's a 'situation'?

Spaghetti: It's a kind of house.

Ulla: We live in a flat.

Malcolm: We have to be talking about GETTING GIGGLY in a situation.

Janet, the teaching assistant, came and joined Malcolm's group.

Malcolm started to feel very GIGGLY.

'Right!' Mr Keenly called out. 'All eyes to the front.'

Oh no, Malcolm thought. Our Talk Group hasn't even begun to talk about GETTING GIGGLY.

'What have we got?' said Mr Keenly.

'I've got 50p,' said Ulla.

Janet put her hand on top of Ulla's hand and said, 'That's nice,' to her, and then pointed at Mr Keenly.

Ulla doesn't always quite get it, Malcolm thought, but neither do I. Or anyone. And that's the point, he thought.

All of us don't always quite get it, Malcolm thought. If Uncle Gobb got it that no one gets all of it, it wouldn't be so horrible being with Uncle Gobb. And then, all of a sudden it was like the clouds opened and a great big face with a great big voice said in an American accent,

'THAT'S THE BIT THAT UNCLE GOBB DOESN'T GET. HE DOESN'T GET IT THAT NO ONE GETS ALL OF IT.'

Malcolm smiled.

Mr Keenly said, 'Malcolm, you're smiling. What's your GETTING GIGGLY thing?'

Everyone went very quiet.

The whole class looked at Malcolm. He started to say the first thing that came into his head which was the stuff about Uncle Gobb and this great big moment with the cloud opening … but then he quickly realised that that had nothing to do with GETTING GIGGLY.

He looked at Janet.

He remembered that what made him GIGGLY was Janet. Well, not just Janet. It was the fact that Janet and Mr Keenly liked each other.

The class was still quiet.

The whole class was still looking at Malcolm.

Then he said, 'You and Janet.'

The whole class took in a big breath at the same time. It was a massive whole-class gasp.

GASP!!!

A gasp big enough to swallow the Niagara Falls, if you were in America, Malcolm thought.

Usually, the gasps big enough to swallow the Niagara Falls only happened when someone was in **BIG TROUBLE**. Like the time Humpty brought some sick to school. Humpty isn't his real name.

So Malcolm knew he was in **BIG TROUBLE**.

Crackersnacker whispered, 'You did that Blurting-Out Thing there, Ponkyboy.'

Crackersnacker had once told Malcolm that he did Blurting Out quite often, and that sometimes it would be better if he didn't.

That was Crackersnacker's **'HELPFUL ADVICE'** and, just like the Helpful Advice in this book, was free.

Even the whole Ponkyboy thing came about because of Blurting Out. That was the time when Malcolm was thinking about 'Inky Pinky Ponky,' at the very moment he was on TV being asked 'What is the capital of Italy' and he said, '**Ponky!**' That was such a

Great Big Blurting Out, the whole world knew about it.

And now he had done another Blurting Out and the whole class was looking at him.

Getting giggly

Mr Keenly started to speak.

I know what's coming, thought Malcolm. I'm going to have to go and see Mrs Office and she'll ask me to say sorry and then she'll ask me why I'm sorry and I won't know why I'm sorry. I never know why I'm sorry. And that's when things go fizzy.

And when things go fizzy, I feel sad.

'That's very good, Malcolm,' said Mr Keenly. 'That's exactly the kind of situation we're talking about.'

'We live in a flat,' Ulla said.

'That's nice,' said Janet.

Mrs Office walked in. With her were two men and two women in suits.

'And that just about finishes that,' said Mr

Keenly smiling very nicely at everyone.

Malcolm was puzzled. How did 'that' just about finish 'that'? What finished what? They had hardly started to talk about GETTING GIGGLY. And this was supposed to be Talk Time when they talked about Important Things. That was their Learning Objective.

But now it had all ended. Just because Mrs Office and the two men and the two women in suits walked in.

'They've come to arrest us,' Crackersnacker said.

'No,' said Malcolm, 'I think they've come to do the leak.'

'No,' said Crackersnacker, 'the people

who come to do leaks wear blue overalls.'

'Right, everybody,' said Mrs Office. 'I want to introduce you to some people who are going to have a lot to do with the school. They've come from the Gobb Education Force.'

The four people did some big smiling. And nodding.

Malcolm heard 'Gobb Education Force' like it was a baked bean in a spoonful of vanilla ice cream. Odd, brown and very, very surprising. How could these people be part of the Gobb Education Thing?

One of them started speaking.

Malcolm looked at Crackersnacker. It was amazing. The man was almost certainly speaking English but the only words that Malcolm and Crackersnacker could understand were 'the' and 'and'. One more word that Malcolm heard was the word 'inspection' though he wasn't sure he understood it.

Malcolm looked at Crackersnacker.

'They're not coming to arrest us, Crackersnacker. I think they've come to do some inspection.'

When Malcolm said 'inspection', he did the Mr Keenly thing where he opened his eyes wide, said a word with big lips, and made a little wiggly finger sign as if he was underlining the word.

What happened next was an Awkward Silence.

This is where things are pretty silent and everyone feels awkward.

BLAH BLAH BLAH ETC
BLAH BLAH BLAH
BLAH BLAH ETC
INSPECTION...
BLAH BLAH

Like when you're on a bus and you say, 'Mum, someone's done one,' and everyone hears and they think you mean that someone did a fart, but you didn't mean that, you meant, 'Someone at school has done a picture of the school summer fete' because your mum just asked you if it was you who was supposed to be doing the picture of the school summer fete, so you say, 'Mum, someone's done one.'

And there was an Awkward Silence in the
class right now because no one knew what to do
next.

So the whole class was breathing quietly.
Even Singalong and Freddy, who hardly ever did
anything quietly.

Malcolm was also breathing quietly in the awkward silence but the words 'Gobb Education' were going round and round in his head like the words at the top of a roundabout at the fair.

A roundabout? he thought … and as he thought that, he heard that same voice, in an American accent, saying, 'Hey buddy, over here it's a carousel. Not roundabout. Carousel. Now let's go get some of that cotton candy I promised you …'

CHAPTER 4

Sorry about the name of Chapter Three. Malcolm didn't get to America. Sometimes things don't work out in the way you say they will.

This chapter hasn't got a name in case things don't work out in the right way again. Bad luck can sometimes come in twos.

Or threes. Or ones.

OR WEASELS!

No, not weasels.

3,000 YEARS B.C.   **A WAR**   **KING JOHN**

ou'll remember that the last chapter ended with an Awkward Silence. This chapter begins just as the Awkward Silence comes to an end with:

'The Timeline,' said Mr Keenly.

The Timeline was pinned up round the room. At the beginning of The Timeline it said 3000BC. At the end of The Timeline it said NOW.

In between there were all sorts of dates and next to the dates it said things like 'War', or 'King'.

(Uncle Gobb loved The Timeline. When Malcolm said at tea-time that Mr Keenly had put up The Timeline round the Malcolm's classroom, he ran round the kitchen, jumping up and down, shouting, 'At last, at last, at last!'

'The point is, Tessa,' he said, 'there are millions of people who don't know which comes first, and which comes second, and which comes third. What comes after first? Second! What comes after second? Third! Everyone needs to know this. They know it in China.'

'A lot of things happen where the third thing comes before the first thing,' Malcolm said. 'Like getting up, having things to eat and going to bed.'

'What?!!!' said Uncle Gobb very crossly.

'Well,' said Malcolm, 'we say that first we get up, then we have things to eat, then later, we go to bed. But if you look at it another way, you could say, first we go to bed, then we get up and then we have things to eat.'

'WHAT???!!!' said Uncle Gobb even more crossly.

Malcolm noticed that a lot of conversations he had with Uncle Gobb ended with Uncle Gobb saying, 'WHAT???!!!'

It was at moments like this that Malcolm loved to imagine a different kind of conversation at home; one that could just end with a 'Mmmm' or a 'Hah!' That would be nice.)

'I want you all to write down in your Timeline Books,' Mr Keenly said, 'the time and place you would most like to have been alive.'

The Gobb Education people wrote something on their clipboards.

There was some hubbub while people couldn't find their Timeline Books but Janet moved round the class like a red-hot arrow finding Timeline Books. The Timeline Books were quite easy to find because they had the words 'Timeline Book, provided by the Timeline Corporation' on them.

Malcolm wrote down, 'I would like to be in America around about the time when my dad went there.'

'Right, all eyes to the front,' said Mr Keenly. 'What have you got?'

'50p' said Ulla.

'That's nice,' said Janet.

The children read out their answers.

'I would like to be in Victorian times because I would say to Oliver Twist that he could have more cornflakes,' said Oliver.

'I would like to be in the Stone Age because I like the Rolling Stones,' said Singalong.

'I would like to be in the Great Plague because I would like to have a great plague,' said Freddy.

Malcolm read out his:

'I would like to be in America when …'

… and he stopped.

He didn't want to say the thing about his dad.

He looked at Crackersnacker. Crackersnacker had that don't-do-a-Blurting-Out-Thing look on his face.

Crackersnacker tried to think of something that he could say to Malcolm to help him. He had seen what Malcolm had written in his Timeline Book, and he could see that Malcolm didn't want to say that.

Then Crackersnacker got it.

He whispered to Malcolm, 'When Clint

Eastwood got out of Alcatraz.'

'... when Clint Eastwood got out of Alcatraz,' said Malcolm, 'the only prison in the United States that no one ever got out of ... apart from Clint Eastwood ... and Alcatraz is an island in the middle of San Francisco Bay,' Malcolm added.

The inspecting people from Gobb Education Force were still writing on their clipboards.

Mr Keenly said, 'What you need to be telling me are the times you would like to be in, taken from OUR Timeline … Oliver – Victorians, very good; Freddy – Great Plague, very good; Singalong, I think you've got your Stones a bit muddled; Malcolm, no Alcatraz in America on our Timeline, I'm afraid.'

(Quite a lot of big eyes, and wiggly underlining fingers went on there.)

etting
iggly

'Excuse me, Mr Keenly,' Crackersnacker said, 'the thing is, Malcolm's got to get to America.'

Malcolm had stopped listening. He was staring at some tiny writing on the bottom of the back page of the Timeline Book. It said:

Of course it does, he thought. It's just like at home, when Uncle Gobb starts firing off questions and facts about spiders and stuff. Now it's Timeline questions. Uncle Gobb was coming

at him from all directions. It felt like Uncle Gobb
had got hold of his head and was squeezing it
harder and harder and harder.

'Well,' said Mr Keenly in one big rush …
(Note: That means you have to say what Mr
Keenly says next, really, really quickly. On your
marks, get set, go!)

'I'm sure we all want to go to America, but Malcolm, you wouldn't be able to go to Alcatraz when Clint Eastwood was there ... that was a film ... it wasn't real ... No. Yes. I mean Alcatraz is real. It was real. But Clint Eastwood wasn't in Alcatraz. That was a story. About the only man ever to have escaped from Alcatraz. If that's true. And Alcatraz is still there. People go. You can go in a boat. I've been there. Ha! Imagine? Someone on the boat fell off. It was awful. Look, let's hear some of the other answers ...'

Malcolm thought that Mr Keenly was getting fizzy. Everyone else could see that the people in suits from the Gobb Education Force were making Mr Keenly VERY, VERY nervous, so they tried to help. They all said that they wanted to know about the boat, Mr Keenly's trip to Alcatraz and the awful thing that happened. This just made Mr Keenly even more nervous because he thought that going to Alcatraz wasn't what they were supposed to be doing. It wasn't THE TIMELINE and it wasn't the Learning Objective.

'All eyes to the front,' said Mr Keenly. 'The bit of The Timeline that we're going to focus on this term is the Stone Age.'

He pointed at the bit of The Timeline on the wall that said, 'Stone Age', and he did more eyebrows, wiggly fingers, underlining words thing.

Singalong said, 'My granddad used to do electricity for the Rolling Stones.'

Mr Keenly switched on the whiteboard and there was a picture of a pile of stones.

Malcolm felt prickly – that feeling you get when things aren't going quite right. They're nearly right and if you could do something to get them more right, you wouldn't feel prickly. Like there are little tiny pins sticking into the back of your neck. Not painful pins. Just prickly pins.

No, there are no such things as weaselly pins.

The thing is, Malcolm thought, we were nearly going to talk about America. America was in the air all round them. You could almost touch America. But something in the room meant that suddenly we couldn't talk about America. It looked like Mr Keenly wanted to talk about America. Crackersnacker had been really helpful. But then it just … slipped away.

I know, he thought, I'll have to have another big conversation with Crackersnacker about my *Dreamy Stuff*, and how to get to America and how we're going to get rid of Uncle Gobb in America, because it's not going to happen here in school.

'Now these stones …' Mr Keenly was

saying … and Malcolm was imagining going home that night and Uncle Gobb saying, 'You did the Stone Age in school today? Right, how many rocks where there in the Stone Age? What were the names of the rocks? How heavy were the rocks?'

Mr Keenly carried on: '... these stones may not look like the most interesting stones in the world, but ...'

... but let's interrupt Mr Keenly there. Let's not carry on with the stones, eh?

Let's leave the stones alone.

Mr Keenly was going to say something that he hoped would make the Inspection People very pleased. He was going to say that these stones are fascinating stones and really, really, really amazing.

(Note: Some fascinating stones turn up in a book called 'Fascinating and Really, Really, Really Amazing Piles of Stones in the Stone Age' written by a very, very close friend of Uncle Gobb called Jack Rock, but that book is not this book.

Sorry.)

CHAPTER 5

The Green Room (Which Is Not Green)
(This Chapter Contains Some Secret
Information About Genies That Has Never
Been Revealed Before. Use It Sensibly.)

If you have read a book called Uncle Gobb and the **DREAD SHED** you will know that if Malcolm rubs his nose, a Genie will appear. If you know this, you may be wondering why he doesn't rub his nose to find out how to get to America. Please don't be impatient. Malcolm does things in his own way and in his own time. He doesn't like being rushed.

If you have read that book, you will also know that if Uncle Gobb polishes his face and says some special words, Uncle Gobb's Genie, Doctor Roop the Doop, doop dee doop, will appear. If so, you may be wondering, hey – if the Genies haven't been summoned by Malcolm and Uncle Gobb so far in this book, what are the Genies doing?

Here now is the secret information about Genies that has never been revealed before: what Genies do when they are in between the times they appear is sit about in a Green Room waiting to be called. You sometimes see a Green Room on chat shows. It's where the guests wait before they come on.

Malcolm's Genie was sitting in the Genies' Green Room.

Uncle Gobb's Genie, Doctor Roop the Doop is NOT in the Genies' Green Room.

So where is he? What is he doing? And why?

We're not the only ones to wonder about all this.

Malcolm's Genie wants to know. He wants

to know so that next time he's summoned, any information he's collected about Doctor Roop will help Malcolm. That's what a good Genie does: gets the info on his master's enemies.

But how will Malcolm's Genie get this info?

He will have to stop staring at himself in the Green Room mirror, saying to himself, 'I like the haircut, Mr Nice Guy,' right now.

He will have to stop making his biceps bulge while saying, 'Grrrrrrrrrrrr!' right now.

He will have to focus on helping Malcolm.

Now, there's one other thing I didn't say about Green Rooms. They're great places for gossip. Genies chat.

Even as Malcolm's Genie was waving his scimitar in the air, and shouting, 'I'm so accurate with this, in one swipe I could cut the wings off a passing fly ...' he heard someone say, '... Doctor Roop the Doop ...'

'Aha!' he said to himself. 'Info in the air, eh?'

Cunningly, he pretended not to have heard and went on swiping and swooshing with his scimitar while he listened to the gossip.

Old Tom, a Genie who was not very fit, was always a bit out of breath and had to send excuse notes to his master when he was summoned, was talking to Sandy the Demon Giggler. She was known as the Demon Giggler because her giggling was so dangerous it could make Presidents and Prime Ministers feel a bit silly.

'… he's got his own private helicopter,' said Old Tom.

'He hasn't,' said Sandy.

'He has.'

Malcolm's Genie did some quick thinking. Uncle Gobb's Genie, Doctor Roop the Doop has his own private helicopter? This was serious gossip. No Genie has his own private helicopter. How come Uncle Gobb's Genie did? He swished his scimitar while carefully not looking at Old Tom and Sandy.

'Gobb wants everyone to answer questions properly,' said Old Tom.

'I know,' said Sandy.

'No, not just Malcolm. Everyone.'

'That's impossible.'

'That's so everyone will end up thinking in the Gobb way,' said Tom.

'That's impossible too.'

Next time Malcolm summoned him, he would have to tell him all this. It was all more dangerous than he thought. He swished his scimitar even faster.

Swish! Swish! Swish!

But Old Tom had some more gossip.

He leant forward and made his voice go quiet.

Malcolm's Genie stopped swishing.

Old Tom said, 'The thing is, Uncle Gobb knows that Malcolm is messing up his plans. But

Uncle Gobb hasn't figured out that the thing that makes Malcolm strong is his great friend Crackersnacker. It's the power of the two of them working together that gives him the big problem.'

'I see where you're going with this,' said Sandy. 'Gobb doesn't know, but Doctor Roop the Doop DOES!'

'Yes indeedy,' said Old Tom, 'Doctor Roop the Doop is desperate to tell Uncle Gobb that he needs to split up Malcolm and Crackersnacker. That's the key to everything.'

'Apart from my front door,' said Sandy and started one of her Demon Giggles.

All this gossiping and giggling set

Malcolm's Genie off again with his scimitar.

Swish! Swish! Swish! went the scimitar.

'Hey, careful what you're doing with that, pal,' said Old Tom as he and Sandy made off to the Genies' table tennis room to have a game of table tennis.

The thing is, Malcolm's Genie thought, does anyone else know this stuff?

This is a mystery that is yet to unfold.

Here is a picture of a mystery unfolding.

Suddenly, Malcolm's Genie felt himself being tugged out of the Green Room window, up into the sky.

Malcolm had summoned him.

BYE!

CHAPTER 6

A Short Chapter
(This Is A Short Chapter Because Malcolm Is
Not Very Comfortable And We Don't Want To
Leave Him Being Uncomfortable For Too Long.)

Malcolm didn't want Uncle Gobb to hear or see what he was doing so he was under his bed where he was uncomfortable.

The Genie arrived, as usual, through Malcolm's nose.

'Nice landing, big boy,' he said to himself.

To Malcolm, he said, 'I am the Genie of Malcolm's Magic Nose, your wish is my wish …

no, sorry, my command is … oh, I mean …'

Malcolm whispered, 'Never mind all that. It's great you've come. Listen – '

'No, you listen,' said the Genie.

'No, you listen,' said Malcolm. 'I need you to help me to get to America.'

'Sorry, pal, I don't do flying carpets any more. They're not allowed by air traffic control,' said the Genie.

'No, no, I mean I need you to think up some plan that will get me and Uncle Gobb to America, so that I can leave him there, and I can meet my dad again and sort it all out.'

'Hmmm, I usually do heavyweight stuff; throwing tables, that sort of thing.'

'You're not very good, are you?' said Malcolm.

'I've got an excellent six pack,' said the Genie.

It was all quiet under the bed for a bit, until the Genie said, 'But if I were you, I would go and see Brenda.'

Malcolm thought about Brenda, Dad's sister.

Why would she be able to help him get to America? He wasn't even sure that Brenda much liked Malcolm's dad.

(Don't worry that you don't know much about Brenda yet. You will.)

'And I've been looking out for useful info

for you,' the Genie said.

'Oh, thanks,' said Malcolm still thinking about Brenda.

'The stuff you need to know is this: Uncle Gobb's Genie, Doctor Roop the Doop, has figured out that it's the power of you and Crackersnacker working together that's stopping Uncle Gobb from changing everyone's minds so they think like him. So Doctor Roop the Doop is dying to tell Uncle Gobb that bit of info so that he can pull you two apart. But he can't, until Uncle Gobb calls him up. See?'

Hmmm, Malcolm thought. So here's me thinking how I'm going to get rid of Uncle Gobb, but if Doctor Roop the Doop gets to tell

Uncle Gobb that Uncle Gobb has got to break up me and Crackersnacker, we're in trouble. I'm going to have be very cunning. In America. When we find Dad … if we can get there …

'Thanks, Genie of My Nose,' he said, finally.

As Malcolm didn't seem to need him for anything else, his Genie headed back to the Genies' Green Room.

CHAPTER 7

Where Is Houston? Who Is Houston?

In the school playground, Malcolm and Crackersnacker were taking it in turns to sit on a football. This was a game they had invented to do with who could do the best wiggling on the ball without falling off. It was a kind of opposite of 'keepy-uppies'. More like 'keepy-downies.'

They gave each other marks.

'Six!'

'Oh c'mon! That was a seven!'

'No, you put your hand on the ground.

You lose marks for that.'

'OK!'

Crackersnacker had been doing some hard thinking about Malcolm and his dad. So, while they were resting from wiggling on the ball, Crackersnacker said, 'You could tell your mum you want to see your dad.'

Then the bell went.

After school, that evening, Malcolm sat on his favourite bit of the floor in the sitting room and poked it with his finger. Mum walked in and out, moving tea cups. Malcolm wasn't sure if Mum knew that she did this or not. She walked in, moved a tea cup two inches one way and walked out. Then she walked back in and moved the tea cup the two inches back to where it had been.

'Can we go and see Dad?' Malcolm said.

It was the Blurting-Out Thing.

Mum went straight to the window. Malcolm wondered if his father had turned up at that very moment, outside the window.

'Malcolm,' said his mum, 'I try very hard to do things right. I really do. If you really, really

want to see your father, then I will try to do what I can. The thing is, we're short of cash. You know what that means, don't you? Mm? If we say, "Right, it's a good idea to go and see your father," that means we'll have to do some big thinking about how we're going to get the cash to go.'

'What I'm thinking ...' Malcolm began

to say, but at that very moment, they both heard the front door slam. It was Uncle Gobb. So very quickly, before he walked in to the room, Malcolm said, 'We could talk to Brenda.'

'Brenda?' said Mum, and in walked Uncle Gobb.

'Britannia!' he said. 'Britannia socks! I've been talking with my friends at The Cow Club and we agree that what Malcolm needs are Britannia socks.'

Mum and Malcolm looked at him.

Uncle Gobb wasn't looking at either Mum or Malcolm. He was looking ahead of himself to some distant place that wasn't actually there because there was a wall in the way.

Mum shook her head as if she was trying to get the brains inside lined up in the right way to make out what Uncle Gobb was saying. That's because she was also thinking about Brenda. She put that to one side and answered Uncle Gobb.

'We haven't got any Britannia socks,' she said.

'And that's it!' said Uncle Gobb. 'Of course we haven't. That's the problem, Tessa. Why do you think things don't work? Why do you think it's all falling apart? I'VE BEEN TO CHINA. Why do you think we have people running around thinking all sorts of things that they shouldn't be thinking? Mm?'

'Because I'm not wearing Britannia

socks?' Malcolm said.

'Yes, good, Malcolm. Very good. Finally, Tess, I'm getting through to the boy.'

'What are Britannia socks?' Malcolm said.

A look of amazement mixed with contempt appeared on Uncle Gobb's face.

'Oh for goodness sake. One moment, it seemed as if you knew why and how Britannia socks would solve the problem; I was full of hope for the future and everything was looking good; then the next, it's obvious that you don't have a clue what Britannia socks are and … I'm in despair. You are hopeless, Malcolm. Completely hopeless. You are going to fail, Malcolm. You are going to fail.'

At this, Uncle Gobb sat down, slumped forward and put his head in his hands, saying, 'Fail, fail, fail, fail, fail, fail …'

If ever there was a time when Malcolm felt strongly that his dad had to come rushing through the door to take him away, it was now. Or even better, Dad would swap places with Uncle Gobb. Some kind of magic could turn Uncle Gobb into Dad, like some digital morphing thing. And it could happen now.

Now, now, now, now, now, now, now, now, now, now, now, now, now.

All these nows started whirring round inside his head like candyfloss in the candyfloss machine. Or cotton candy.

'Derek,' said Mum, 'why don't you pop upstairs to your room and do some nice little pictures of your little Britannia socks?'

'Yes,' said Uncle Gobb, 'that's good. That's very good. You're looking good, Houston,' and Uncle Gobb skipped out the room.

'Houston?' said Malcolm, 'Who's Houston?'

From outside, Malcolm heard Uncle Gobb let out a scream. In the middle of the scream, he heard Uncle Gobb shout, '"WHO'S Houston?" he said. "WHO"?! I wasn't talking about a PERSON called Houston! The boy doesn't even know it should be

"WHERE is Houston?"'! Houston is a PLACE! Don't they do geography any more?'

'Where is Houston?' Malcolm said to his mum.

'In America,' Mum said.

'Dad lives in America all the time now, doesn't he?' Malcolm said.

Mum went over to Malcolm and stroked his hair. He was looking at the table wondering what Britannia socks look like so he didn't see that she was crying.

CHAPTER 8

Far And Few

'Today,' said Mr Keenly, 'we're going to do a poem.'

The inspectors from the Gobb Education Force immediately started writing things down in their notebooks. Were they going to be here all week, all year, all century? Malcolm wondered.

'The poem is called "The Jumblies".'

'I love raspberry jumbly,' said Ulla.

'That's raspberry jelly,' said Janet nicely.

'"The Jumblies" is a poem by a man called Edward Lear and I want you to find out all the information you can about Edward Lear and "The Jumblies".'

JUMP FORWARD (a bit like a flashback but the other way)

We jump forward to the moment when Malcolm and Crackersnacker have written down their Information About Edward Lear.

Edward Lear

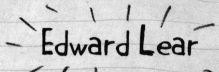

by Malcolm and Crackersnacker

In the nineteenth century, Edward Lear had twenty brothers and sisters. If he had one more, they would have been two football teams.

Edward Lear's mother was very tired and Edward Lear grew a very, very, very big beard. He didn't grow this beard when he was very young. Later, Edward Lear liked to draw parrots. Even later, Edward Lear wrote poems. Some of them he put in *A Book of Bosh*.

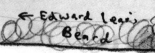

Edward
LEAR →

← Edward Lear's
Beard

No one knows what 'Bosh' is. Sometimes when people say that they've done something really quickly, they say, 'And that's it: bish bash bosh.'

Edward Lear did not write a book called *A Book of Bish Bash Bosh* but maybe when he got to the end of his book, *A Book of Bosh*, he said, 'And now that's the end of *A Book of Bosh*: bish bash bosh.'

Here is part of 'The Jumblies' by Edward Lear:

Far and few, far and few
Are the lands where the Jumblies live.
Their heads are green, and their hands are blue,
And they went to sea in a sieve.

A sieve is a thing with holes in.
Nearly everything has holes in, eventually.

The Jumblies sailed away in
their sieve for a year and
a day and then they came
back in their sieve.

The End

Malcolm loved the Jumblies. Everyone said they shouldn't sail away but they did. Then they came back. Well done, Jumblies.

When he got home that night he told Mum and Uncle Gobb he had been doing a poem.

Uncle Gobb said, 'But did you learn it? Did you learn it off by heart?'

Malcolm tried to think if he had learned it.

'Er … we … er read it,' he said, then he started getting excited. 'And Crackersnacker and me found out loads and loads about Edw–'

But Uncle Gobb didn't want to know.

'See that Tessa? That's what's wrong. He didn't learn it off by heart and he isn't learning it off by heart now for homework. I despair.'

He slumped forward, his head landing on the table.

Well, his head would have landed on the table if there hadn't been a slice of toast and strawberry jam on the table. So, in actual fact, he slumped forward on to a slice of toast and strawberry jam.

When he sat up, the slice of toast and strawberry jam was sticking to his face.

'You've got a slice of toast and strawberry jam sticking to your face,' Malcolm said.

'I KNOW!!!!' shouted Uncle Gobb.

'Put the toast in the bin, Derek,' said Mum, 'then pop up to the bathroom and clean yourself up, mm?'

Uncle Gobb stormed out, shouting, 'I WASN'T TALKING ABOUT TOAST. I WAS TALKING ABOUT LEARNING POEMS OFF BY HEART. BUT NOBODY LISTENS TO ME IN THIS PLACE.'

... which was a shame, because what Mum said was good advice.

If ever you find that you've got a piece of toast and strawberry jam sticking to your face, peel it off and pop to the bathroom and clean yourself up.

See? I told you there would be good advice in this book.

So do I, thought the dog.

CHAPTER 9

The Raisin

Brenda the Mender wasn't in.

I mean, she wasn't in when Malcolm and his mum went to see her after Malcolm came home from school. Brenda was out the back. Out the back was where she kept cogs, ratchets, pulleys, batteries, coils, flanges, brackets, bolts, tacks, raisins, springs, hinges, joints, valves, pistons, piston rings, cam shafts …

Raisins?

While she was mending washing machines, phones, hearing aids, umbrellas, remote-control model cars, electric mobility cars – including her own, gas cookers, toasters, windows ... and, well, anything really ... she liked snacking and the thing she most liked snacking on was raisins. Brenda's daughter Wenda was in charge of the raisins.

'Aha,' said Brenda to Wenda. 'You're the raisin why.'

'Not laughing,' Wenda said.

'Now, Tess,' Brenda said. 'I have air miles … could you pass me that knurled nut?'

Wenda offered Malcolm a raisin.

'Thanks,' Malcolm said.

'You're welcome,' Wenda said, and went back to her sudoku puzzle.

Malcolm ate the raisin.

Brenda was talking about air miles because Mum and Brenda had talked on the phone about America.

'But for three of us,' Mum said, 'that would be hundreds of thousands of air miles.'

'I have millions,' Brenda said, 'and don't ask me how or why I have millions. I just do.'

AIR MILES INFORMATION

An air mile is an imaginary present. You buy something or you spend some money and some people called 'Air Miles' tell you you've got some air miles. Every now and then 'Air Miles' tell you that if you've got ten thousand air miles you can go somewhere.

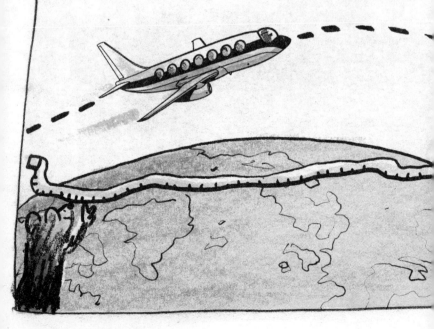

WARNING

If you've got ten thousand air miles, that doesn't mean that you can go somewhere ten thousand miles away.

You can go about 569 miles away.

ANYWAY. Brenda the Mender had millions of air miles. Millions and millions of air miles. Don't ask how or why.

'And another thing,' Brenda said. 'I think Wenda and I will come too. I'd like to see that flibbertegibbet too. Va va vroom!'

'It's "Va va voom",' said Wenda.

'Where I come from, it's "Va va vroom",' said Brenda.

'You'll have to leave your cogs and pulleys at home,' Mum said.

'Can we leave that brother of yours at home too?' Brenda said.

'No, no,' said Malcolm. 'We have to take Uncle Gobb. We have to. We really have to.'

A MOMENT FOR US TO
THINK ABOUT THINGS

Is this a strange thing for Malcolm to say?

No.

Because Malcolm's plan is to leave Uncle Gobb in America. That is his Getting Rid of Uncle Gobb Plan.

But – uh-uh – we also know – and Malcolm knows – that Doctor Roop the Doop wants to tell Uncle Gobb how it's Malcolm and Crackersnacker working together that stops Uncle Gobb from getting everybody answering questions in the way that he wants them to. America might just be the place where Uncle

Gobb will summon Doctor Roop the Doop, and Doctor Roop the Doop tells him all this …

END OF THE MOMENT FOR US
TO THINK ABOUT THINGS

Later they had raisin pie.

Malcolm was thinking about the flibbertegibbet. Aunty Brenda must have meant Dad. Why did she call him a flibbertegibbet? What is a flibbertegibbet?

Wenda looked Malcolm straight in the face and said, 'Do your feet smell?'

'No, I don't think so,' Malcolm said as hopefully as he could.

'Good,' said Wenda. 'Because in America people travel about in camper vans. You can't spend days and days in a camper van with someone who has smelly feet.'

Malcolm looked at his feet.

'Do you know where he is?' Wenda asked him.

'He's at home,' Malcolm said.

'No, not Uncle Gobb,' Wenda said. 'I meant your dad.'

'That's enough, Wenda,' Brenda said, not wanting Wenda to talk so directly about Malcolm's dad.

'Do we, Mum?' Malcolm said. 'Do we know where Dad is?'

'Connecticut,' she said and she looked out the window.

Just outside the window was a big face made out of cogs and pulleys and bolts. It was painted green. 'Their heads are green ...' It must be a Jumbly, Malcolm thought.

'Far and few, far and few,' he said.

'What did he say?' said Brenda.

'Their hands are blue,' Wenda said.

'What?' said Brenda. 'Mm? What are you two on about?'

Malcolm's mum was flicking over the pages in her diary. Or her address book. Or both. To and fro. Dates. Addresses. Addresses. Dates. Flick, flick, flick, flick, flick.

For the first time in ages, Malcolm felt calm and good. They were going to go to America. He'd get to see Dad AND get rid of Uncle Gobb. This was better than brown sauce – which Malcolm loved.

The one bit worrying him was whether Doctor Roop the Doop would get to Uncle Gobb to tell Uncle Gobb that he had to do something horrible to break up him and Crackersnacker …

CHAPTER 10

Sorted

Uncle Gobb said that he wasn't going to America.

'I love America,' he said. 'I love the way it's open. It's open all the time. Everywhere. Everywhere's open. And everyone. Everyone's open. And everything's open.'

'If you like it so much, why don't you want to

come?' Mum asked Uncle Gobb.

'America and I are not getting on very well at the moment,' Uncle Gobb said.

Malcolm could feel the whole plan of leaving Uncle Gobb in America going very badly wrong.

'Mind you,' said Uncle Gobb, 'I do have some business to sort out in America ...'

Sort it, sort it, Malcolm said to himself over and over again.

'We'd be going to find Malcolm's dad,' Mum said.

Uncle Gobb said, 'Is that absolutely necessary?'

'I don't know what's necessary and not

necessary any more,' Mum said, slowly winding herself up like a cat about to jump at a mouse. 'All I know is that I look after Malcolm, I look after you. I look after Malcolm because no one else is looking after him. I look after you because you can't look after yourself. Oh yes, and when I've got a moment, I look after myself.'

Uncle Gobb listened. Then he said, 'I go round to Mr Iqbal's and get the baked beans when you ask me to.'

'Yes, you do, you do,' Mum said. She stopped being a cat getting ready to catch a mouse. 'But you don't know how to look after yourself. So if you don't come, we can't go. And Malcolm doesn't get to see his dad.'

Uncle Gobb thought some more.

'You said the Brenda woman is coming,' Uncle Gobb said. 'Does that mean Wenda's coming too?'

'Yes,' said Mum.

'That makes more people who don't know how to answer questions properly,' said Uncle Gobb.

This conversation was reminding Malcolm of the Uncle Gobb conversation about the baked beans with him and Crackersnacker.

CRACKERSNACKER?????!!!!!!

Oh no, if Crackersnacker stayed at home, and if Uncle Gobb summoned Doctor Roop the Doop and if Doctor Roop the Doop told Uncle Gobb how him and Crackersnacker have to be broken up … Uncle Gobb would send Doctor Roop the Doop to do something terrible to Crackersnacker … Oh no, he couldn't leave his best, bestest, bestest ever, most bestest ever everest friend behind. Crackersnacker so totally had to come. Then they could keep an eye on Uncle Gobb in case he tried to break them up …

until he swapped Uncle Gobb with Dad.

'Mum, Crackersnacker,' was all he said.

'Crackersnacker?!' said Uncle Gobb. 'That frightful little worm? He's not worth the paper he's written on.'

'He's not written on paper,' Malcolm said.

'Your Crackersnacker is one of the reasons why we're going downhill,' Uncle Gobb said.

Malcolm looked at Mum. Mum looked at Malcolm.

'If we have the air miles, Crackersnacker can come too,' she said. 'I am crazy. I am seriously the craziest person in the universe. What am I letting myself in for?'

Uncle Gobb narrowed his eyes. He did this when he was planning something.

'I warn you now, you two,' he said. 'On this trip I'm going to be exceedingly busy with business.'

'Yes, Derek, I'm sure you will,' Mum said, 'but in the meantime, why don't you go and put some underpants in your suitcase? Last time we went away, you forgot to pack any.'

CHAPTER 11

Ber-lamm Ber-lamm Ber-lamm

After school, when Malcolm and Crackersnacker walked in through the door of Malcolm's place, Mum was waiting for them.

'Crackersnacker can't come,' Malcolm blurted, 'I can see it. I can see it on your face.'

'Wait for it, Malcolm,' Mum said.

'There's no point in waiting for it. I can see it. I don't want you to tell me. I know, I know, I know,' Malcolm said and put his hands over his ears, shut his eyes and put his head on the table.

Malcolm's Mum looked at Cracker-snacker and said, 'Me and you will have a talk then.'

'I've been to see your mother,' Mum said to Crackersnacker, 'and –'

'**DON'T SAY IT!**,' shouted Malcolm with tears in his eyes. 'I don't want to hear you say, "Crackersnacker can't come to America."'

'I won't say it,' Mum said. 'What I'll say instead is that he CAN come to America.'

Malcolm didn't hear that, because now he was saying, 'Ber-lamm, ber-lamm, ber-lamm,' and rubbing his ears very violently.

Crackersnacker punched the air, slapped his right knee and spun round very quickly.

Malcolm didn't see that because he had his eyes shut.

The dog saw it.

(What the dog didn't know was where it was going to go, while everyone was in America. Don't worry. The dog went next door where it was given loads of 'TIDDLES'. Tiddles are tasty treats.)

Malcolm went on thinking that Crackersnacker wasn't going to America for another two and a half minutes. When he finally got the point that Crackersnacker WAS going, he got cross that he was the last to find out.

Later, when they were having tea, Uncle Gobb suddenly stood up and said, 'Tessa, I think the time has come for me to inform the boys why

and how it used to be better.'

'What did?' Malcolm asked him.

'Ice cream,' said Cracker-snacker before Uncle Gobb could answer. 'I was talking to a man on the bus and he said that they don't make ice cream the way they used to.'

'I like ice cream,' Malcolm said, 'I don't see how it could be better.'

'Excuse me,' Uncle Gobb said, beginning to sound irritated, 'I'm talking about things that are much more important than ice cream. I'm talking about heritage.'

Because of the way Uncle Gobb spoke, Malcolm thought he said he was talking about 'Hairy Titch'.

'Who's Hairy Titch?' he said.

HAIRY TITCH

'It's "heritage",' Uncle Gobb said.

But Malcolm thought it sounded like 'Hairy Titch' again, so he said, 'I know, yes, that's what I said.'

'No,' said Uncle Gobb, 'you said "Hairy Titch".'

'No,' said Malcolm, 'it was you who said, "Hairy Titch", not me. There's a little kid in our

school we call "Titch" but he isn't hairy.'

'No,' said Crackersnacker, 'he hasn't got a beard.'

Uncle Gobb walked over to the door and got ready to leave the room.

'All I'm trying to do here, Tessa, is inch these two idiots forward on the great chessboard of life.'

Then he left the room.

I thought Uncle Gobb was going to tell us about Hairy Titch, Malcolm said to himself, but then suddenly he switched over to talking about chess. Anyway, we're not idiots. Dad wouldn't call us idiots.

Later, in the bedroom, with Malcolm in bed and Crackersnacker on the floor, they whispered to each other in the dark about where they could leave Uncle Gobb when they were in America.

'Hollywood.'

'*The Simpsons* ...
you know ... the place ...
erm ... Springfield.'

'The White House.'

'The museum in
Night at the Museum.'

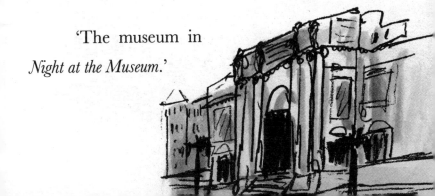

As you can see, it had turned into saying the first American place each of them could think of, whether the place existed or not.

'The elevator.'

'Elevator?'

'That's the American word for a lift.'

'I know it is – what elevator?'

'I don't know what elevator. Any elevator.'

Malcolm dozed off

thinking that the plan was good. There were so
many places to leave Uncle Gobb. America is

CHAPTER 12

A Very Similar Conversation

Uncle Gobb was polishing his face and muttering, 'Italy, Spittaly, Spain was Hungary, Spain ate Turkey dipped in Greece.'

Over and over again.

What was going
wrong? Why wasn't his
Genie appearing?

Once more.

There was a
flash, and into Uncle
Gobb's room came
Doctor Roop the Doop,
doop dee doop.

'What kept you?'
Uncle Gobb asked him
crossly.

'I thought that
one of the rotor blades
on my helicopter was
faulty.'

'Was it?'

'No.'

'You were wrong then. Hah! But you know everything,' said Uncle Gobb.

'Well, I didn't know that,' said Doctor Roop.

'What?' said Uncle Gobb.

'Well, if I knew what, I would know. But the whole point is that I don't know.'

This wasn't getting anywhere so Uncle Gobb thought he would get on with what was on his mind.

'We're going to America,' he said.

'I know,' said Doctor Roop.

'I have a plan,' said Uncle Gobb.

'So do I,' said Doctor Roop.

'My plan is to get rid of Malcolm and Crackersnacker, put them somewhere out of my sight,' said Uncle Gobb.

'No,' said Doctor Roop, 'too drastic. Either you or I will end up in prison. I've got a better plan.'

But Uncle Gobb wasn't listening.

'How am I going to rid of them?' said Uncle Gobb.

'I don't know,' said Doctor Roop, 'but all you need to do is separate them. They get their power when they're together. We have to break that.'

Uncle Gobb still wasn't listening.

'I tried the **DREAD SHED**, but it didn't work. And anyway, I can't take the **DREAD SHED** to America, can I?' said Uncle Gobb.

'No, nay, verily,' said Doctor Roop talking for a moment in his favourite old-book voice, 'you can't. No room on the plane.'

'So let's do some forward planning here, Doctor Roop,' said Uncle Gobb, 'let's think first of WHERE I can get rid of them. What about … er … Hollywood?'

They took it in turns to think of places.

'*The Simpsons* … you know … the place … erm … Springfield,' said Doctor Roop.

'The White House.'

'The museum in *Night at the Museum*.'

As you can see, it had turned into saying the first American place each of them could think of, whether the place existed or not.

'The elevator.'

'Elevator?'

'That's the American word for a lift.'

'I know it is – what elevator?'

'I don't know what elevator. Any elevator.'

Uncle Gobb held up his hand.

'Go away and think about it, Doctor. Next time I call for you, make sure you've got a plan.'

'I do have a plan,' said Doctor Roop.

'I don't want YOUR plan. I want you to work out a plan to make MY plan work,' said Uncle Gobb.

And because Genies have to do what their masters tell them, Doctor Roop the Doop couldn't tell Uncle Gobb his plan to break up Malcolm and Crackersnacker, which would have helped Uncle Gobb get everyone to answer questions properly and think like him.

NOTE ON CHAPTER TWELVE

You probably noticed that some of the things that people said in Chapter Twelve were very similar to things that people said in Chapter Eleven. I noticed that too.

CHAPTER 13

The Tree Trolley

At the end of term, Mr Keenly said he hoped that they would all have a great summer. Malcolm noticed that Janet looked at Mr Keenly and said that she was looking forward to having a great summer too. And she did the eyebrow, wiggly finger underlining thing when she said 'great summer'.

On the plane to Boston, Uncle Gobb started talking about a tea party. Malcolm was getting dozy but just before he fell asleep, he was pretty sure that he heard Uncle Gobb

say that people in Boston pour their tea into the harbour. Could that be true?

When he woke up, Uncle Gobb was still talking. This time he was saying that no one was allowed to say 'camper van'.

'Don't say 'camper van',' he said.

'But we're hiring a camper van,' Mum said.

'In America it's called a Winnebago,'

Uncle Gobb said. 'A Winnebago. A Winnebago. It's the wrong word but it's what they say here.'

'That's enough now, Derek,' Mum said. 'Remember the deep breathing I told you to do when you get excited.'

A woman called Wilma met them at the airport with the Winnebago.

Crackersnacker said, 'Wouldn't it be great if her name was Winnie, then she could be Winnie Bago?'

Malcolm and Crackersnacker practised saying, 'Hi, I'm Winnie Bago and this is your Winnebago.'

Brenda drove the Winnebago out of Massachusetts into Connecticut.

Mum, Crackersnacker, Malcolm, Brenda, Wenda and Uncle Gobb were singing:

'Far and few, far and few
Are the lands where the Jumblies live.
Their heads are green, and their hands are blue,
And they went to sea in a sieve.'

Wenda gave a raisin each to everyone.

'Pumping gas,' Crackersnacker said.

He was practising American things to say.

'I hope you're not,' Wenda said.

'No, it doesn't mean what you think it means,' he said. 'It means getting petrol out of the petrol pump and putting it in your car.'

'As if!' Wenda said.

'You do know where we're going, don't you, Tessa?' Uncle Gobb asked.

'It's a summer camp,' said Mum. 'I told you before.'

Malcolm was feeling a bit fizzy.

Mum shouted, 'Look, there's an ostrich farm.'

They all looked out the window. They couldn't see any ostriches. Just a huge sign that said, 'Lucky Joe's Ostrich Farm'.

'Not far now,' Mum said.

About ten minutes later they arrived at a place that had a sign on it that said:

'THE   '

They hadn't finished making the sign.

'This is it,' Mum said.

Malcolm's legs started to feel wobbly.

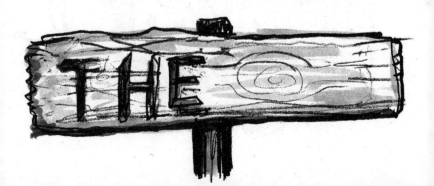

This is where I'm going to meet Dad again and everything's going to work out perfectly, he thought. At last, at last, at last.

Everyone got out. As Mum had said, it was a camp, with a mix of huts and tents. Children of all ages were wandering about. Most of them had mud painted on their faces. One walked up and said, 'Hey!'

Mum said, 'Excuse me, is Fender here?'

'Sure,' said the girl and she went on standing there.

'Do you know where he is?' Mum said.

'Nope,' said the girl who was now picking some of the mud off her face.

'I'm here!' a voice called out from a tree.

There was a loud whoop and suddenly a man wearing nothing but a pair of shorts flew out of the tree, sitting on a trolley fixed to a wire and shot past them.

'It's fixed, guys!' he shouted, which caused what looked like hundreds of children (it was 15 actually) to appear out of the huts and tents screaming to get a go on the tree trolley.

The man got off the trolley and walked towards them. Malcolm was shaking. The man had mud on his face too but Malcolm could see that it was Dad.

Next thing, he had picked up Malcolm, and was shouting, 'Wow, you've grown some, Malky!'

Then, turning to the others, he said, 'And sheesh, it's Brenda the Mender. Whoa, Sis!' and he did high fives with Brenda. He put Malcolm down, picked up Wenda and said, imitating an English accent, 'Is it Wenda the menda?'

'No, I don't do the mending,' Wenda said.

Dad pinched her cheek, saying 'That's from your Uncle Fender', and then he looked at

Crackersnacker.

'And you're Malky's buddy?'

Crackersnacker said, 'Sure,' in a nearly-American accent.

He got a joke punch on the shoulder for that.

Then Dad looked at Mum and Uncle Gobb. He looked and he looked.

'Tess,' he said, 'this is what it's like.'

And Uncle Gobb said in a sneery voice, 'Oh yes, we can all see what it's like here, Fender.'

Malcolm heard himself breathing. It was all so sudden. And loud. And big. And full of not knowing what was going to happen next.

I'm Malky, he thought. That's who I am here.

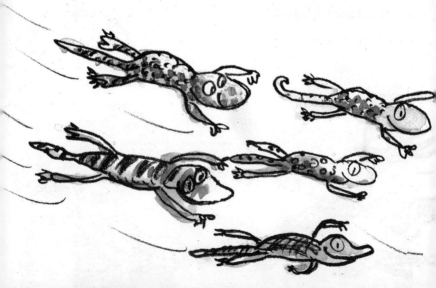

CHAPTER 14

Ah! Yeah!

The girl who first met them said that her name was Lizard. Malcolm guessed that was because she said she was doing a project on lizards. She took Malcolm, Crackersnacker, and Wenda to see her lizards. Then she showed them how to do the Lizard Crawl, which meant wriggling face down in the mud.

Malcolm kept looking round to see where Dad and the others were but they had gone off to a hut to talk.

He wondered whether anything was being sorted.

Was Dad going to come back home with him and Mum?

And how could he and Crackersnacker find somewhere to leave Uncle Gobb?

And had Uncle Gobb called up Doctor Roop the Doop?

Later, Dad came and found them, looked at the lizards and said to them, 'Cool, huh?'

Then he said to Malcolm, 'Hey Malky, let's talk.'

Next thing, Malcolm and Dad were walking in the woods, talking.

Malcolm had planned this. He had a speech ready and nothing was going to stop him. So he said to Dad, 'What's going to happen is that you and Uncle Gobb are going to change places, swap over. Uncle Gobb is going to come here to America and you're coming to live with me and Mum. What do you, think?'

Dad seemed surprised.

'Ah, well, whoa there, buddy,' he said. 'It's not quite as easy as that. You see, I haven't talked to you about my projects …'

'Like Lizard and her lizards?' Malcolm said.

'Well, yes,' said Dad. 'Like that, in a way. You see, I run a string of these places,' he said.

'OK not just yet I don't, but I'm hoping to. You see, Malky, it could all be just taking off. And this means, buddy, that I can't let the whole thing drop.'

Taking off? Whole thing drop? Malcolm wasn't sure if he was getting what Dad meant. Was Dad saying that he wasn't going to come back with them? Malcolm felt a deep, deep sadness was just round the corner waiting to come along and grab him.

'Look, Malcolm,' Dad said, 'Tess and I both love you to bits. We do, we do. And, hey, who knows what might happen later? But right now, this, this …' He waved at the trees all around them. '… This is something that I've got to grab with both hands.'

Later? When was 'later'? Later today? A hundred years time? Malcolm could feel the tears in his eyes.

'What about Uncle Gobb, though?' he said.

What he meant to say, was, how can I go on putting up with horrible, awful, nightmarish Uncle Gobb? You need to do something …

But he didn't say that.

Dad said, 'Look, Malky, I can imagine just how bad it is. I know Derek is a pain. But … how can I say this? Derek is … like … ill. Things have gone badly wrong for him. I mean, over here, in America. Not only with Tammy, you know, his wife?'

'Yes,' Malcolm said, 'I know about that and how it all went

'Well,' Dad said, 'that wasn't the only thing that went blammmm … the whole Gobb

Education thing … just as it was taking off, right here in America, it was taken off him.'

Malcolm started to feel fizzy. It was taking off … then it was taken off???

Dad went on: 'There's a seriously big guy over here ... let's call him Joe Big, and him and Uncle Gobb were doing stuff together ... all that Gobb Education thing ... and then suddenly Joe Big said he could do it without Uncle Gobb ... and he did! He took it off him ... but, get this, Joe Big kept the Gobb name. Because Gobb sounds kinda funky ...'

Dad let the story fade away into the woods.

Malcolm wondered how you could steal someone's name.

Dad went on explaining: 'When all this happened, your Uncle Gobb went into a **RAGE**. And it went on and on and on.

Remember, it was your mum who was looking after him, huh?'

'Yes,' said Malcolm who, for the first time, wondered if in some sort of a way he, Malcolm, looked after Uncle Gobb too.

Dad said, 'I couldn't do what your mum does with Uncle Gobb, buddy. And anyway, to be honest, I don't like the stuff that Joe Big and Uncle Gobb are into. All those questions, and the Gobb Education Force. I'm into these summer projects.'

Malcolm tried not to cry.

It felt hopeless and useless and didn't make sense. Hopeless, useless and senseless. He would have to tell it all again to Crackersnacker to get Crackersnacker to explain whether it meant what he was afraid it meant.

'Anyway,' Malcolm said, taking a deep breath, 'if you can't take Uncle Gobb, is there some way you can stop him from coming back with us, and then, you … er … the swap thing … erm … ?'

'Ah! Yeah!' said Dad. 'That's … yeah … I'm going to get my head round that one.'

All of a sudden, that sounded a bit better. There was a little tiny bit of hope there. Like, even when you think you think you've finished a plate of baked beans, there's one bean left, hiding behind the crust you didn't eat.

CHAPTER 15

Ah! Yeah!

Not long after, Dad went for a walk in the woods with Uncle Gobb.

Uncle Gobb had some explaining to do as well. 'Life, Fender,' he said, 'is becoming impossible with Malcolm. Well, not only Malcolm. It's Crackersnacker too. I'm going to have to tell you very directly, Fender: you have to keep Malcolm here in America. And another thing. Crackersnacker and Malcolm – it's as if they're stuck together with superglue. I'm thinking you have to take Crackersnacker too. I can tell you,' he added, 'Tessa's at the end of her tether. Malcolm is your son, Fender. You have to stand up straight, look at life in the eye and do right. Take the boy. And the other boy.'

Uncle Gobb had prepared this speech in his room after Tess had sent him to bed.

Dad replied with, 'Ah! Yeah! That's ... yeah ... I'm going to get my head round that one.'

Uncle Gobb was amazed to hear Dad answering by saying things that seemed to agree with what he had just said.

Superb, thought Uncle Gobb. I am such a good talker. I am so good at getting people to agree with me, I could talk the strawberries out of strawberry jam.

Eeek!

STRAWB JAM

NOTE ON CHAPTER FIFTEEN

Yet again, we find that something that happened in one chapter has happened again in the next. Did you notice that? I did.

CHAPTER 16

The Tower At The End Of The World
(Or Is It The World At The End
Of The Tower?)
(Or Is It The End Of The Tower
Of The World?)

By now it was evening, everyone in the camp ate sausages and beans apart from the people who didn't eat sausages. They ate beans.

The camp leader for the day – she was called Ocean – said that the plan tonight was to do The Scary Tower Trip.

Everyone who was going on the trip said, 'Wooooo!!!!' which Malcolm reckoned meant that they had done this sort of thing before. The people not going on the trip thought about how lucky they were not going on the trip.

'These woods,' said Ocean, 'once belonged to a woman called Laetitia von Bildungsroman who was so rich she put diamonds in the teeth of her pet snake. Over there …' Ocean waved over there.

'… is Laetitia von Bildungsroman's huge house and Tower. Let's go!'

Some people said, 'Wooooo!!!' again, then along with Malcolm, Crackersnacker, Uncle Gobb, Wenda, Lizard and Mum, they headed off through the woods. After some mumbling and stumbling, they could see, looming up above the trees, Laetitia von Bildungsroman's Tower.

The way to say 'Laetitia' is 'Let-isha'. A bit like
lettuce with a 'sha' on the end.

That was some more **HELPFUL INFORMATION**.

'In this Tower,' said Ocean, 'there are
some stairs. You go up the stairs and there are
landings. On the landings there are doors. If you
go through the doors into the rooms and it works
out well for you, you could become the Camp
Octopus and wear the octopus mask and the
extra legs all day long. One last thing: (Ocean
leant forward, did a big stare at everyone) the
best room is at the top.'

Aha, I know what that means, Malcolm

thought. That's where Dad and Uncle Gobb ARE going to swap over. That's why he said 'later'. And that's why it's Ocean saying all this, not Dad. Dad's up the top of the Tower.

Aha, I know what that means, Uncle Gobb thought. That's where Fender is going to take Malcolm and Crackersnacker. Of course – that's why it's Ocean saying all this, not Fender. Fender's up the top of the Tower.

Inside the Tower it was empty and whispery.

Everyone said, 'Wooooooo!!!' and the Tower echoed back; 'Woooo!!' Ocean said, 'Best of luck in there. You'll need it.'

Then she laughed a spooky movie laugh.

Up the empty, whispery steps they climbed.

Up and up and up and round and round inside the Tower.

Malcolm looked over the banisters down to the bottom. It was like a twisty eye down there. He felt dizzy. Uncle Gobb looked over the banisters down to the bottom too. When everyone else looked down they said, 'Woooo!'

Lizard grabbed Wenda's hand and said, 'I love this place,' and they headed up the stairs on their own.

Then it was the landing. And a door. And then a room …

Malcolm was thinking that it was getting a bit risky. What if Uncle Gobb called up Doctor Roop the Doop who then told Uncle Gobb to split up Crackersnacker and him in some horrible way, ON THE WAY UP? No time to wait; the best thing to do is try to get rid of Uncle Gobb BEFORE they got there!

Only one thing for it: he had to call up his Genie. He looked around. There were some curtains. He slipped behind them with Crackersnacker and started rubbing his nose.

Malcolm's Genie arrived through Malcolm's nose, carrying some weights.

'I was in the gym, when you called me. I'm upping the reps.'

'What?' said Malcolm.

'I'm increasing my repetitions with the weights,' he said. 'But anyway, what's happening? I am the Genie of the Magic –'

'Never mind that,' said Malcolm. 'I've got to get rid of Uncle Gobb NOW before he tries anything. This Tower feels like a great place to lock him up or something, so we'll be free of him for when Dad comes home with us …'

'Good one, Ponkyboy,' said Crackersnacker.

'Hmmm, best place for that will be in the little room at the top,' said Malcolm's Genie.

'Can you check out what Uncle Gobb is doing now, though? Has Doctor Roop the Doop told him about how he's got to split me and Crackersnacker up? I'm getting worried.'

'I'll do some nosing around,' said the Genie.

'Yes,' said Malcolm, 'but don't just nose. Come up with a plan as well, eh?'

'Yes, yes, yes,' said the Genie. 'I'm not just a pretty face.'

'Pretty face?' said Crackersnacker. 'You've got a pretty face?'

'Oh, one problem, though,' said the Genie. 'I can't just pop back and tell you what I find out, because for some of us weaker Genies, it's too soon to come, go, and come back again. There has to be a gap to build up the power.'

'Oh,' said Malcolm.

'But there's a way round it. If you come across some kind of clue, or message, or some kind of puzzle and you can solve it, that might just pump up enough Genie Juice and I can come back on the strength of it. It all connects.'

'Right,' said Malcolm, and his Genie was gone a second later.

There was a big 'Woooo!!!' from another room. Someone must have found something. Or lost something. Scary Trips are like that.

In another part of the Tower, Uncle Gobb was getting desperate. He was sure that the Tower was the place where he or Fender or both of them were going to get Malcolm and Crackersnacker out of his life, but he couldn't figure out how. And he couldn't risk Malcolm summoning up his Genie. That would ruin everything. Uncle Gobb noticed a door at the end of the room he was in.

I know, he thought, I won't wait till we get to the top. I'll go in there, summon up Doctor Roop the Doop, and ask him to handle it. He could whisk the two boys off, jam them in some little room here and lock them in. Maybe that's what Ocean meant about how the room at the top is the best … Fender must have told her to say that, yes … and then I'll be free to get on with my big job of making sure people answer my questions properly. Come on, Derek, he said to himself, you were famous Gobb once, you could be famous Gobb again.

So, Uncle Gobb slipped through the little door and immediately began polishing his face and saying the magic words.

Sure enough, Doctor Roop the Doop arrived. But because Uncle Gobb hadn't listened to him last time, Doctor Roop was a bit sulky.

Eh? Eh?
Eh?

'Yep?'

Uncle Gobb was excited.

'Now's the time, Roopy. They're both here, we're heading up a tower, up to the top, the little room, what about it? What do you think? Eh? Eh? Eh?'

Did you see that 'Eh? Eh? Eh?'

That 'Eh? Eh? Eh?' meant that Uncle Gobb was thinking that Doctor Roop the Doop should do the locking up thing …

BOOKS DON'T GET NASTIER THAN THIS.

CHAPTER 17

Nasty

If it's all getting too nasty, put this book down now.

If you think you can cope, don't put this book down.

CHAPTER 18

HIGH FIVES!!!!

'Never mind, "Eh? Eh? Eh?"' said Doctor Roop the Doop (who knew exactly what 'Eh? Eh? Eh?' meant). 'I've told you: WE CAN'T JUST GET RID OF THEM!!! We'll end up in PRISON!!!! What we have to do is …'

But Uncle Gobb wasn't listening. You see, Uncle Gobb not only knew all the questions, he also knew all the answers. Someone who knows all the answers thinks he doesn't have to listen to some old wrinkly Genie with glasses rattling on about his own plans.

'… And I'm telling you,' said Uncle Gobb, 'this Tower is the place where we can get rid of the boys, I mean really, really get them out of my life. Then I get my powers back. This is my moment. This is going to be …

THE GOBB TOWER
OF POWER!!!'

Uncle Gobb started puffing himself up, his eyes were gleaming and his mouth was wiggling about like two snakes having a fight.

'Ha-haaaaaaaa!'

roared Uncle Gobb triumphantly.

This made Doctor Roop the Doop even more annoyed. Not just annoyed; angry. In fact, it made him so angry, he walked out in a big, big, sulk.

INFORMATION ABOUT GENIES

Genies don't do that sort of thing. It's not allowed.

It's against the Genies' Rules.

END OF INFORMATION ABOUT GENIES

But Doctor Roop the Doop did it anyway! He got into his helicopter and off he went.

Unbelievable, but true.

Uncle Gobb was left on his own.

No matter, he thought, I'm getting my old powers back … I can feel it. I can handle this on my own. And he strode back into the room, thinking about a little room at the top the tower with a great big door and loads of locks and bolts and Malcolm and Crackersnacker locked up inside …

A HORRIBLE LOOK
CROSSED UNCLE GOBB'S FACE.

If the dog had been there, he wouldn't have liked that look.

Meanwhile, Malcolm and Crackersnacker were still climbing. As they climbed, Crackersnacker chanted, 'Far and few, far and few …' like it was a marching song, to help them keep going.

They got to another landing and went into the next room. At one end of the room was a screen with a picture on it of some strange creatures with green heads and blue hands.

A sign said, 'Help. We don't know who we are. We don't know what we're doing and we don't know why we're doing it. If you can tell us, maybe you will become the Camp Octopus.'

Next to the screen there was a microphone with a message on it saying, 'Tell us.'

So Malcolm spoke into the microphone, 'You're Jumblies.'

Crackersnacker leaned in and said, 'Yeah, Ponkyboy is right.'

'And you've gone to sea in a sieve,' Malcolm said.

'And me and Ponkyboy don't know why you've done that because a sieve lets in water,' said Crackersnacker.

'But you got there and back OK,' Malcolm said.

'Yeah,' said Crackersnacker.

'We thought that was good,' Malcolm said. 'To get there and back in a sieve was brave.'

'We liked that,' Crackersnacker said.

'And you're a bit like us,' Malcolm said. 'We've gone away …'

'And we're going back,' said Crackersnacker looking at Malcolm.

Malcolm reckoned that this could it be just the kind of puzzle solving that could bring back his Genie.

But was it?

CHAPTER 19

It Was

I t was.

(Which you knew, because that's the name of the chapter.)

CHAPTER 20

Mega, Massive Or Mammoth?

Malcolm's Genie bustled in.

'Did you see the way I bustled in?' he said.

'Yes,' said Malcolm. 'That was good bustling in. Felt better than when you come out of my nose.'

'You did that, guys. Well done. You cracked that puzzle really well.'

Malcolm and Crackersnacker got a proud feeling.

The Genie went on, 'I am the Genie of the Magic –'

'Never mind that,' said Malcolm.

'Fair enough,' said the Genie. 'On with my amazing news, then. I've been nosing around and I have seen something "extraordinaire".' (Which means 'extraordinary' in French. More Helpful Information there.)

Malcolm's Genie cleared his throat and announced, 'Doctor Roop the Doop, doop dee doop, has walked out on Uncle Gobb. He has broken the Genies' rules and gone. Left him.'

What?!!!!

Malcolm and Crackersnacker looked at each other with very big eyes.

Was this good, or what?! Or was it totally good? Amazing? Mega? Massive? Mammoth?

(Note: Mr Keenly would know if it was mammoth because mammoths lived in the Stone Age.)

'Crackersnacker,' said Malcolm excitedly, 'this is even bigger than mammoth!

UNCLE GOBB HAS NO GENIE TO HELP HIM!!!

That means he doesn't know that the one thing he's got to do is to split me and you up.'

'Wow,' said Crackersnacker quietly, 'wow, wow and wow again.'

Malcolm could feel his heart thumping away like a heart going very fast. Which it was. It was going to be much easier now to do the Dad/Uncle Gobb swap at the top of the tower.

Then he and Crackersnacker walked out of the room and on up the stairs, leaving the Genie behind while he checked his cheek muscles in the little hand mirror that he always carried around with him.

Malcolm and Crackersnacker looked down. There was Uncle Gobb, climbing, stopping, panting, gasping, trying to climb some more, stopping, his chest heaving, his face sweating, hoping that his

KOF!
PANT!
PUFF!

big moment was coming at the top of the Tower.

Suddenly, Malcolm thought that Uncle Gobb looked very small. And very weak. Just a little Uncle Gobb. Who wasn't very good at climbing. A little tiny Uncle Gobb who had no Doctor Roop the Doop to help him. Just a little Uncle Gobb who shouts questions that people didn't want to answer. A little Uncle Gobb whose name was on all these education things but only because Joe Big stole his name off him.

Malcolm could feel the big swap moment was just a few moments away. This is the 'later' that Dad meant, he thought.

After much more climbing and singing 'Far and few …' Malcolm and Crackersnacker reached the top of Laetitia von Bildungsroman's Tower.

Wenda and Lizard and Mum were already there. They all looked out of the windows, over what seemed like the whole of America.

Far, far below they could see the woods, the lights in the camp and even the tree trolley, but not the lizards, it was too dark. Malcolm felt good. At any moment now, the swap would happen, and Uncle Gobb had no Doctor Roop to stop it happening. Where was Dad?

What seemed like ages later, Uncle Gobb arrived, gasping and panting. And panting and gasping.

'Now – (gasp) – now – (pant) – I'm – (gasp gasp) – going to get – you two – (pant pant) – OUT OF MY LIFE!'

'No you're not, Uncle Gobb,' said Malcolm. 'You're out of breath.'

'Sit down and get your breath back, Derek,' Mum said, 'before you do any more talking.'

'Have a raisin,' said Wenda.

'Look at my lizard,' said Lizard, taking a lizard out of her pocket.

Uncle Gobb was too much out of breath even to eat a raisin, or look at a lizard. All he could do was sit down and puff.

Malcolm knew at that moment, even though Dad wasn't there, they had won this part of his struggle. He and Crackersnacker gave each other high fives. And high tens for luck.

And, wahay! Malcolm knew that it was only because Mr Keenly had told them about the Jumblies and that him and Crackersnacker had liked the Jumblies so much that they had been able to solve the Jumblies puzzle. And they knew that it was because they had solved the puzzle that Malcolm's Genie could come back. And it was because he could come back, they heard that Doctor Roop the Doop had left Uncle Gobb. And they knew that without Doctor Roop the Doop, Uncle Gobb never got to hear that the one thing he needed to do was come up with a way to split up Malcolm and Crackersnacker. And now, because he didn't do that, he was nothing more than … than … a little Gobb.

A little Gobb.

Hah! That's a win, Malcolm thought. A victory, for us.

Yes.

I mean

YES!!!!

MORE HIGH FIVES!!!

Then Malcolm looked round. He thought, now, surely this is the moment when Dad does something that means that Uncle Gobb will stay here and not come back with us??? The swap …???

Where is Dad? Malcolm thought.

Where is Fender? Uncle Gobb thought.

CHAPTER 21

A Sad Chapter That Is Very Short In Order To Make Sure The Sad Stuff Doesn't Last Too Long

Dad wasn't there.

CHAPTER 22

Where Things Seem To Be Not Quite So Sad

Malcolm thought some more: OK, then Dad will be at the bottom. Things are still going to work out because Uncle Gobb hasn't got Doctor Roop the Doop to help him.

Uncle Gobb thought some more: Fender will be at the bottom. Things are still going to work out.

So, along with the others, Malcolm and Uncle Gobb headed down the stairs.

CHAPTER 23

Can Two People Be An Octopus?
Can An Octopus Be Two People?

When they all got to the bottom, Malcolm looked for Dad.

But there was only Ocean.

No matter, he'll turn up in a moment, Malcolm thought.

Ocean was very excited about the way Malcolm and Crackersnacker had done the puzzle.

'We heard you on the sound

system back at base,' she said. 'You two are the Camp Octopus.'

'How can two people be an octopus?' said Malcolm.

'Two arms each, two legs each … makes eight,' said Crackersnacker. 'Like an octopus.'

But where was Dad?

Malcolm asked Mum and Mum asked Ocean.

'Oh, right, yeah,' said Ocean. 'Fender left a message. I'll read it: Big news. A place has come up in some woods in Maryland. Some kind of forest ranger's hut. I've got to go there right now, or we might lose it. It looks like we can make another one of these camps there.'

Malcolm looked at the ground.

'We're growing!' Ocean said excitedly. 'Oh yeah, and Fender says here, I'm looking forward to seeing you, Malcolm, very soon. As soon as possible.'

Crackersnacker put his arm round Malcolm.

He needed that.

Crackersnacker looked at his great friend Malcolm. He could see from his face that he was sad. It had gone wrong.

'The thing is, Malky,' said Crackersnacker, 'I think the way it is … is … in the middle of good things, there are sometimes … erm … things that are not so good.'

They thought about that.

'I know what it is!' Malcolm said. 'It's like we said in our Edward Lear information thing: everything gets holes in eventually.'

They smiled.

'Hey,' said Crackersnacker in his American voice, 'and don't forget: the Jumblies got there, AND got back, even though the sieve had holes in.'

'Yeah,' said Malcolm trying to feel hopeful. 'And we can come back here, can't we, Mum?'

There was a groaning sound.

It came from Uncle Gobb. Nothing had worked out well for him. No Fender, no Genie, no swap. And no one to answer questions correctly.

Mum waited for Uncle Gobb to stop groaning and then she answered Malcolm's question: 'Yes, we can, Malcolm.'

That was good, Malcolm thought. And meanwhile, there's Mum, there's me and there's Uncle Gobb, but there's one BIG difference. Uncle Gobb has lost his Genie. Doctor Roop the

Doop has left him. Uncle Gobb won't dare to be anywhere near so bossy from now on.

Weasels: From now on? Hang on, does that mean that there's going to be another book about Malcolm, Crackersnacker and Uncle Gobb?

Weasel: I don't know. I'm just a weasel.

Weasels: And Brenda and Fender?

Weasel: I don't know. I'm just a weasel.

Weasels: And Wenda and Lizard?

Weasel: I don't know. I'm just a weasel.

Do YOU know?

A TEST

INSTRUCTIONS

You have 45 seconds to complete this test. When you see a question, read it and then write your answer in the space provided, provided there is a space provided. Do not eat this test.

You should work through the test until you are asked to stop. When you are asked to stop, stop. This means that you should stop writing. It doesn't mean that you should stop breathing. Don't stop breathing. And don't stop blinking. Blinking is useful. Actually, breathing is useful too.

If you finish before the end, go back and check your work. When we say 'go back' that doesn't mean 'go back towards the back of the room'.

You've taken up at least 20 seconds reading this, so now you have less than 45 seconds to answer the questions in this booklet.

Ha!

QUESTIONS

1. What is the answer?

2. Is the sun?

3. Underline the verb in the sentence: 'The verb scored a great goal.'

4. There were two boys: Pete and Re-peat. Pete left the room. Who was left?

5. There were two boys: Pete and Re-peat. Pete left the room. Who was left?

6. There were two boys: Pete and ... OK, we'll stop doing this now.

7. What does 'the' mean?

8. Where do the knives and forks go on

a times table?

9. What is the next question?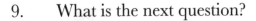

10. Is this

    a) the next question,

    b) this question or

    c) the last question?

11. A train left the station at 10.00 a.m. It travelled for one hour and arrived at the next station at 9.00 a.m. How fast was it going?

12. Underline the right answer.

13. Put this in the correct order: sky, bus pass, melon, toenail.

14. Billy is wearing a blue hat.

a) What colour is the hat?

b) It is raining. Why is Billy wearing the hat? If you write 'Because he supports Chelsea' (or any other football team that wears blue), you are wrong.

15. Write the next number in this sequence: 451, 9, 9, 9, a number, another number, 23

16. Have you finished this test?

17. Match the following by drawing lines between a word in the left hand column with something else.

The national anthem

16 carrots

Goldilocks

An eyebrow

Plastic sausages

18. Hello?

19. Everything is a solid, a liquid or a gas. What is the opposite of a solid? Only one answer is correct. Er ... actually, that may not be true. Answer the question anyway.

20. Where's Wally?

ACKNOWLEDGEMENTS

We would like to thank the weasels for making such an enormous effort to come along and appear in this book. Most weasels aren't anywhere near as kind or as hard-working as the weasels in this book. We would also like to

thank the relatives of Laetitia von Bildungsroman for allowing us to use her tower. No character in *Uncle Gobb and*

weasels being WEASELLY

MORE weasels being WEASELLY

PROFILES

Michael Rosen

Michael was born and brought up in a flat but this didn't make him flat. He is not flat. He now lives in a house that isn't a flat, and the house isn't flat either. In fact, so far nothing in this profile of Michael Rosen is flat. Now here comes a flat bit. When Michael sings, he often sings flat. That means singing a tiny bit too low. Like when you want to go for a walk under the sofa but it's too low. Michael has never walked under a sofa.

Neal Layton

Neal started drawing, painting and writing a long time ago. Not as long ago as the Romans. Or the Saxons. Or the Normans. The Romans, Saxons and Normans wore helmets. Neal does not wear a helmet, not even when he's drawing, painting and writing. You could say that Neal is an artist. You could also say that because he draws he's a drawer. The trouble with saying that, though, is that you might think he's someone who lives in a chest of drawers. Neal does have a chest but that doesn't mean that he's a chest of drawers.

DEFINITIONS

America A film about a place called America

Genie A magic helper that sounds like the girl's name 'Jeanie'

Green Room A room that is not green

Jeanie A girl's name that sounds like 'Genie'

Leaning Objective What you hope to get

out of leaning on someone

Learning Objective What happens if you object to doing any learning

Lizard A four-legged animal called a lizard

Mud Wet earth that has become muddy

Muddle When someone falls in mud

End of Definitions The part of the Definitions where it ends

INDEX

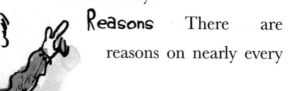

page … Or did I mean 'raisins'? Ah yes, I meant 'raisins'. There aren't as many raisins as there are reasons but there are too many of them to list them here.

Squirrels 🐿 Weasel: I think you mean 'weasels'.

No, I meant squirrels.

🐿 Weasel: Are there any squirrels in this book?

No.

The Stone Age The Stone Age can't be in this book because it was the Stone Age and this isn't the Stone Age, it's some other kind of Age. Maybe it's the Cauliflower Age. In fact, the Stone Age was such a long time ago, they didn't even have paper. This book is made of paper, so that's another reason why the Stone Age isn't in the book. In the Stone Age they sooooo didn't have paper, they only had stones. Their clothes were really uncomfortable because they were made of stones too

Make sure you
haven't missed

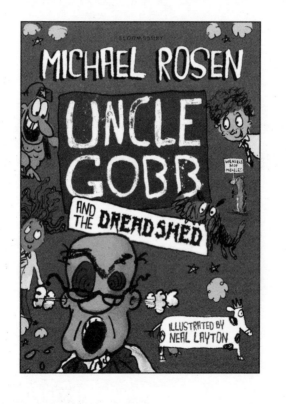